My Big Rig

written by
Jonathan London

illustrated by
Viviana Garofoli

Marshall Cavendish Children

All rights reserved
Marshall Cavendish Corporation, 99 White Plains Road, Tarrytown, NY 10591
www.marshallcavendish.us

Library of Congress Cataloging-in-Publication Data

London, Jonathan, 1947-
My big rig / by Jonathan London; illustrated by Viviana Garofoli. – 1st ed.
p. cm.
Summary: A boy imagines what it would be like to drive a big rig across the country.
ISBN-13: 978-0-7614-5346-8
[1. Tractor trailers–Fiction. 2. Truck drivers–Fiction. 3. Imagination–Fiction.] I. Garófoli, Viviana, ill. II. Title.

PZ7.L8432My 2007
[E]–dc22

2006022277

The text of this book is set in Futura.
The illustrations are rendered in Adobe Illustrator.
Book design by Vera Soki

Printed in Malaysia
First edition
1 3 5 6 4 2

Marshall Cavendish
Children

For Gerrardo, who loves trucks
— J.L.

For Mela, for trusting in my work
— V.G.

Wouldn't it be fun
to drive a truck
across the country?

CLANG! CLANG!

PUZZLE

I climb into my big rig
and wave good-bye.

I blast my horn.
My engine roars.

My big rig rolls
through the city . . .

across a bridge . . . and out into the country.

My big rig rolls across a valley · · ·

up a mountain . . .

through a tunnel . . .

and down the other side.

ZOOM!

It's time to eat.
I downshift gears,
stop my truck,
and dunk doughnuts
at an all-night truck stop.

It's time to roll.
I climb into my eighteen-wheeler
and hit the road.

My big rig rolls

across the desert . . .

over some mountains . . .
and across the plains.

I talk on my CB.
"What's your handle?"
"Fast Freddy," he answers.
"Keep on truckin', good buddy."
"Roger that," I say. "Over and out!"

My big rig rolls
over the hills . . .
through the forest . . .

and down to the sea.

I unload in the harbor,
down at the docks,
onto the giant
sea-going freighters.

Just in time,
because I hear
my father calling,

"Time for dinner!"

I eat and go to bed.
And my big rig rolls . . .

in my dreams.